Thumbelina,
Tiny Runaway Bride

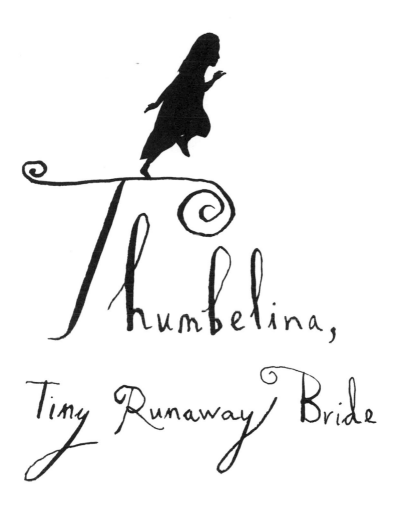

# Thumbelina, Tiny Runaway Bride

by Barbara Ensor

based on the fairy tale by
Hans Christian Andersen

schwartz & wade books · new york

A technical note to readers:
To make it possible for you to read
Thumbelina's tiny handwriting
without special glasses
(which might give you a headache),
we have enlarged it many many many times.

Published by Schwartz & Wade Books, an imprint of Random House Children's Books, a division of Random House, Inc., New York. · This is a work of fiction. Names, characters, places, and incidents either are the product of the author's imagination or are used fictitiously. Any resemblance to actual persons, living or dead, events, or locales is entirely coincidental. · Copyright © 2008 by Barbara Ensor · All rights reserved. · Schwartz & Wade Books and colophon are trademarks of Random House, Inc. · Visit us on the Web! www.randomhouse.com/kids · Educators and librarians, for a variety of teaching tools, visit us at www.randomhouse.com/teachers

Library of Congress Cataloging-in-Publication Data

Ensor, Barbara.
[Tommalise. English]
Thumbelina : tiny runaway bride / Barbara Ensor. — 1st ed.
p. cm.
Summary: In this expanded version of the Andersen fairy tale, a tiny
girl no bigger than a thumb becomes separated from her overprotective
mother, records her feelings in a diary, has adventures with various
animals, and searches for someone to love.
ISBN 978-0-375-83960-3 (trade) — ISBN 978-0-375-93960-0 (lib. bdg.)
[1. Fairy tales. 2. Size—Fiction. 3. Self-reliance—Fiction.
4. Animals—Fiction.] I. Title.

PZ8.E596Th 2008
[Fic]—dc22
2007015684

The text of this book is set in EideticNeo.
The illustrations are rendered in collage, and pen and ink.
Book design by Rachael Cole

PRINTED IN THE UNITED STATES OF AMERICA
10 9 8 7 6 5 4 3 2 1
First Edition

This story was first told by a particular swallow
perched on the windowsill of a particular man,
a man named Hans Christian Andersen.
We know this because that particular man wrote
all of it down—along with a few details of his
own—so the rest of us could hear.
And now it is my turn to tell the story.
Soon it will be yours.

For my brothers and sister,
Paul, David, and Diana, with whom
I spent countless marvelous hours
in the miniature worlds of our
collective imagination.

prologue

# prologue

**H**ow could such a thing happen?

Thumbelina was a friendly and considerate girl, so how *could* she leave bridegroom after bridegroom in the lurch like that? (And just because some of these men were animals in no way excuses it.) Except for her height— exactly one and five-eighths inches in her stocking feet—Thumbelina was a girl very much like you. In fact, you would have been glad to call her your friend.

By his own account, Hans Christian Andersen first heard Thumbelina's story from a swallow that landed on his windowsill in Denmark, about a hundred and seventy-five years ago. He wrote it down, the story was translated into dozens of other languages, and people have scarcely stopped talking about it ever since. What's odd, though, is that for all the talk, hardly anyone seems to remember what actually *happened*. Even with all those books and movies and songs.

If you ask me, Thumbelina's cuteness—her dainty charm and the sheer novelty of her size—has stopped people from taking her seriously. She deserves to be right up there with Romeo's

Juliet, Cinderella, and the Little Mermaid. The pluck and courage with which Thumbelina faced obstacles were extraordinary, even by the standards of people more than two inches tall. I hope this longer version of her story, complete with never-before-published excerpts from her diary, will show her to be so much more than a cute little plaything. Thumbelina can be an *inspiration,* not just to small Scandinavian girls, but to *all* of us, large and small, male and female, all over the world.

Getting to know Thumbelina has changed my perspective in some important ways. Perhaps, as you step into her shoes, it will alter yours too. It might start when you take a second look at a pistachio shell you happen to pick up, to see if it might work for Thumbelina as a bowl. Maybe a kitten that once seemed fluffy and adorable in your eyes will now strike you as menacing, with those vicious claws and sharp teeth. You might even find yourself completely unable to read with the sound of that lawn mower in the background until you have checked to be absolutely sure that any persons of Thumbelina's stature are safely out of harm's way.

Certainly you will discover that Thumbelina's problems were *anything* but small.

For your convenience, we have printed *Thumbelina: Tiny Runaway Bride* as a regular-sized book. And now, dear reader, we are ready to begin.

## chapter 1

Without a father, you can't have a baby—everybody in Denmark knows that, and the whole world as well. And Anne Marie knew it too. But she wanted a baby so badly. She wanted one every minute of every day.

And so she decided to see a witch.

It's not like she didn't know what the risks were—how witches often give you what you ask for technically, but it isn't really what you want. Still, Anne Marie went and knocked on the black door of the gray house that her friends had once pointed out to her on the way to school.

As she waited for someone to answer, Anne Marie considered the terrible things that could happen. Maybe the witch would give her a baby bat and it would eat her, starting with her eyes. Although this was the kind of thought that might make another person run, Anne Marie noticed that her own two feet stayed still.

Just then the door opened and a witch with a pointy hat and a clipboard appeared.

"My fee is twelve kroner, and I do insist on cash up front," she said.

Before handing over such a large sum of money, Anne Marie wanted to be sure the witch could help her.

"I'll listen to what you have to say in a private room," said the witch. "Even though I already know what it is," she muttered to no one in particular.

Anne Marie fished in her pockets for the money. Twelve kroner was more than she had ever spent on anything. It was a lifetime of savings. But compared to jumping into a cauldron of boiling water or chopping off a finger, it didn't seem so bad.

Anne Marie took a seat in the waiting room. A handful of people were already sitting there in silence. Two had covered baskets on their laps, from which small rustling, squeaking, and peeping sounds could be heard.

After attending to a few other matters, the witch came over to Anne Marie, glanced at the clipboard again, and ushered her into a tiny dark room.

Anne Marie knew that this was her one chance to make things clear.

"A baby alligator or even a baby snake is really cute in its own way, but—" she began.

"Miss, I have a lot of other people waiting out there."

Remembering the serious looks on the faces of those people and the odd sounds coming from their baskets, Anne Marie became silent.

"I'm going to give you something," the witch went on. "And listen carefully, because I don't want to have to go through all this again." She sounded like Anne Marie's high school math teacher.

"This may look like a barley seed," said the witch, holding up a single seed for Anne Marie's inspection. "But I assure you it is not.

"First you have to get it safely home without losing it along the way. I know this sounds simple, but not everyone succeeds. Then you . . ." And she proceeded to tell Anne Marie exactly what to do.

As the witch spoke, Anne Marie tried not to imagine the mistakes she might make and where that might lead.

"You don't need to understand why you are doing these things," the witch

explained. "You simply need to do them."
Then she took Anne Marie's money and
escorted her to the front door.

Anne Marie thanked the witch in a
way she hoped was appropriate for the
transaction that had just taken place.

As an extra precaution, she did not
hum or step on a single crack in the
sidewalk on her way home. She didn't
let herself think about anything (not
even the clouds in the sky) except the
witch's instructions.

At home, Anne Marie closed the door behind her, put the seed on the kitchen table, and took a deep breath.

Now, where was the terra-cotta pot with the hole in the bottom?

chapter 2

Anne Marie planted the seed in the moist dark earth, then put the terra-cotta pot with the hole in the bottom on a windowsill in the kitchen. Quite suddenly, two pale green leaves shot up. Anne Marie gasped and then smiled a new kind of smile—one of deep happiness.

That night she dreamed that

her arms were wrapped around a baby.

When Anne Marie woke up, she walked directly to the windowsill.

"Gosh!"

A puffy pink flower with silken petals had appeared on the end of a sturdy stem. Except that its petals were sealed shut like an important letter, the flower looked very much like a tulip.

Anne Marie leaned over and kissed it, which caused a popping sound, a little flash of light, a puff of smoke, and a faint smell of gunpowder.

When the smoke disappeared, she noticed that the petals had unfurled and inside, right at the center, sat a teeny girl on a small green stool. It was a strange sight.

The girl looked to be about three years old and wore a simple white dress.

Anne Marie noticed that the girl was exactly the size of her right thumb.

"Thumbelina!" said Anne Marie, surprised by the musical sound of the name she had just made up.

The tiny girl looked into her eyes with an expression of complete trust and the beginnings of something called love.

Just then, a terrible fear swelled up inside Anne Marie, replacing the ache for a baby that had been there before. *What if something were to hurt this child?* She trembled at the thought and resolved to do everything she could to protect the dear girl.

Thumbelina made a surprising sound for one so small and so young. She sang a note that was high and long, and full of depth. It sounded like nothing ever heard before, yet as familiar as toast.

As Anne Marie looked at the little girl, she felt as though her blood were changing from yellow to red, or all the rivers in Denmark had changed their course so that now they flowed in the opposite direction. It was as though all the compasses had pointed south before, and now they knew to point toward the north pole.

If Anne Marie had ever wondered who she was, she knew now. She was Thumbelina's mother.

And Thumbelina's mother knew just what to do. She took half a walnut shell off a shelf beside the kitchen table and set to work making a cradle for her daughter. She smoothed the outside, rubbed it with lacquer, and filled it with dandelion fuzz to make it soft and warm.

When the cradle was ready, Anne Marie gently lifted her daughter out of the flower and placed her in the walnut-shell bed. Then she covered her darling with three rose petals.

While the tiny child slept, Anne Marie reached for the shoe box she kept on a high bookshelf. Inside were so many things—scraps of cloth, safety pins, plastic jewels, wood shavings— that she had saved diligently for years, not knowing why. With a pair of sharp scissors and a needle and thread, she began to make clothes for her daughter from the small pieces of cotton fabric. They were like dolls' clothes, but much sturdier, and constructed in such a way that Thumbelina could move about. Anne Marie worked quickly and carefully, gluing on a plastic jewel here and a feather there, for effect. Always the dresses had pockets large enough to hold a bow, and toothpick arrows. She made a little notebook too, with a pen and pencil. Soon Thumbelina would practice her letters, and one day she would write down her thoughts and make pictures. In the springtime Anne Marie would look for a small flower that would fit nicely as a hat on her daughter's head.

During the weeks that followed, Anne Marie made a whole world inside their home to replace the dangerous one outside. A boat with tiny horsehair oars waited for Thumbelina, so she could row across a bowl of water. Anne Marie made a bat and ball, a catapult, a chest of drawers, a parachute, a teddy bear. She made a teensy tea set with knives and forks and spoons. And because she knew that her daughter needed her, she felt very happy.

## chapter 3

As Thumbelina grew older, she began to yearn to play outside, where she could feel the moist ground under her feet and the wind and sun against her skin.

"Sorry, Tulip, it's just too dangerous," her mother always said.

But sometimes, if it wasn't "too sunny" or "too windy" or "too rainy" or "too cold," her mother would carefully fence off a little place she'd call a play-

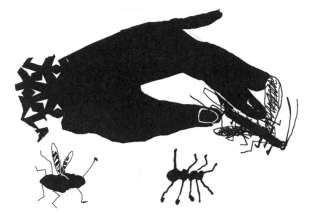

ground. She would always check to see that there were no spiders or beetles, and no small holes her daughter might fall into.

"You just can't be too careful."

Then, and only then, Anne Marie might set Thumbelina down to play, "just for a little while."

Anne Marie taught Thumbelina not to wave at butterflies, because it "encouraged" them. She taught her to say "No!" to snails and turtles that offered rides. And once, when Thumbelina was excited to see children peeking in

through the dining room window, her mother quickly drew the curtains.

"They were staring in the wrong way," she explained.

Anne Marie also taught her daughter her numbers and letters. Thumbelina

memorized the seasons and the names of birds—swallow, bluebird, robin, chickadee—and flowers—rose, honeysuckle, sweet pea, violet.

Soon she was old enough to write in her diary. The special book was always tucked next to her in bed in case she had a dream and needed to write it down the moment she woke up.

Dear Diary,
    I dreamed a worm invited me to explore his underground tunnels.

Even looking through the magnifying glass, it was sometimes impossible for Thumbelina's mother to make out her daughter's tiny handwriting.

Her mother corrected the spelling and wrote comments.

**dreamed**

Dear Diary ↑
I ~~dreemed~~ a worm invited me to explore his underground ~~tunells~~.

**tunnels** ↑

Thanks for larger writing!

Mum

Thumbelina enjoyed sharing her diary with her mother.

One of the grasshoppers invited me to join in a game of <u>leep frog</u>. It was a birthday party and so we all wore hats and there were <u>deelite full</u> party favors to take home...

<u>leapfrog</u>

<u>delightful</u>

But sometimes she sighed to see

*Never speak to strange creatures!!!*

and

*Please do not ever climb under the fence again — for any reason.*

in the margins of the descriptions of her most exciting adventures.

In time, Thumbelina began to address the diary as Dorothy, as though it were a friend.

Thumbelina began to sign all her diary entries with a thumbprint.

Dear Dorothy,
I finally cleaned up my bedroom in the shoe box and put everything away. I do still love my stuffed animals, but I decided to give away a lot of the toys. I wish I could give some of the animals to you. You are my best friend.
Love

chapter 4

A t bedtime Thumbelina's mother often told her exciting stories.

"And then the little girl took an arrow from her pocket and held it up as a warning. And the prickly porcupine curled up into a little ball and stayed that way until she had gone."

Even though the snails and snakes Thumbelina saw from the porch seemed very polite and peace-loving, she was careful to remember her mother's stories just in case "I ever get into a tricky situation."

(Sometimes she almost wished she would.)

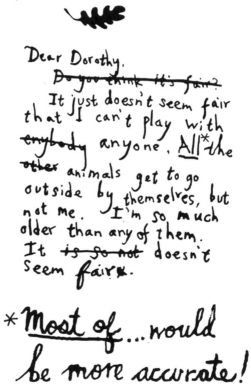

Dear Dorothy,

~~Do you think it's fair?~~
It just doesn't seem fair that ~~I~~ can't play with ~~anybody~~ anyone. All* the ~~other~~ animals get to go outside by themselves, but not me. I'm so much older than any of them. It ~~is so not~~ doesn't seem fair~~s~~.

\* <u>Most of</u> ... would be more accurate!

H

*Dear Thumbelina,*
*Humans take* <u>*much*</u>
*longer to grow up.*
*Love Mum*

As she grew older, Thumbelina stopped writing some of her thoughts down in her diary because they were too private. She was moody on occasion, and her mother didn't always know why.

*I want to do things boys in books do. So what if I scratch my knee or get messy!*

*Does that mean something is wrong with me?*

Thumbelina now begged her mother to let her sleep outside on the porch, "just this one time, please." But it was no good.

"Petal, I've told you so many times."

But then one summer evening, Thumbelina's mother, tired out by all her daughter's begging, finally relented. "Oh, all right, Tulip," she said. "If you're very, very, *very* careful."

*How can I sleep carefully?* thought Thumbelina.

Anne Marie carried the walnut-shell bed to the porch, tucked her daughter under an extra rose petal, and checked to see that the little diary was right beside her. Then she went inside, drew the curtains, and busied herself brewing a cup of mint tea.

Thumbelina felt alive out in the world.

"But I don't have a little light!" she explained when a bunch of young fireflies asked her to join their game.

"That's okay! Please play with us!"

"What are the rules?"

"It's kind of a cross between tag and blindman's bluff."

Soon Thumbelina was dashing around the porch, making crazy shadows dart across the outside of the house.

When a series of flashes from their parents signaled the young fireflies to go home, Thumbelina said goodbye and climbed back into her cozy cradle.

Even
with her eyes
closed she could
feel the bright
moon and stars
tickling her
eyelids.

She knew the river was sparkling nearby, and the nighttime creatures would just be waking up.

chapter 5

Thumbelina hadn't been dozing long when she felt her bed being lifted up. Then it began to hop gently, with her in it, across the porch and down the steps. As it hopped down the hill, Thumbelina caught a whiff of honeysuckle. The air was thick with the sound of crickets chirping.

*What fun to dream I am a rabbit,* she thought.

Thumbelina felt her bed galumphing toward sounds she had only heard from a distance—water lapping against rocks, wind rustling through trees, toads calling to one another in the night. She didn't dare move, even to open her eyes, for fear it would all end.

Suddenly a voice beneath her muttered, "I expect Sylvester will be at home fixing a snack. He'll need some convincing, what with all this hair sprouting out of her head."

Thumbelina lay still, too stunned to make any sense of what she was hearing.

"Can't be helped, though. Worth it

for that bendable waist," the voice continued. "You could really clean behind a stove with one of those!"

Now they had stopped hopping, and Thumbelina sensed that the bed had become stuck. The creature carrying her groaned, perhaps in an effort to dislodge the walnut shell. Thumbelina clutched the shell's edges so she wouldn't be catapulted out.

"Ah, there we go!" cried the voice.

As she felt herself moving through some sort of passage, Thumbelina opened her eyes.

"Ribbet."

She was horrified at the sight of a beady-eyed toad staring straight at her.

"Ta-da!" said the now-familiar voice below her, putting the bed down on the floor. "A bride! For my dearest boy! Isn't she cute, Sylvester?"

Sylvester the toad was looking at Thumbelina with a perplexed and not at all happy expression.

"Well, maybe we can get rid of the hair on top," said his mother, putting a clammy front leg across her son's warty back.

The sight of his warty body made 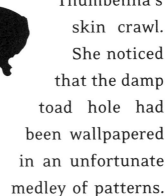 Thumbelina's skin crawl. She noticed that the damp toad hole had been wallpapered in an unfortunate medley of patterns. Mirrors everywhere and linoleum tiles on the floor did nothing to make the place seem any less muddy or dark.

"Oh, Mama, you shouldn't have," protested Sylvester.

"But look, darling—she bends at the waist! No girl toad does that," his mother reasoned. "And can't you just see her following behind and picking up everything you drop!"

The thought of having this toad as a husband made Thumbelina sick to her stomach.

"I can't see you living with one of those toady girls on the other side of the river," continued Sylvester's mother. "Leaving me stuck here, all on my own? I don't think so!"

As the mother toad pointed out how terrific Thumbelina's "jointed claws" would be for tearing the wings and antennae off flies and other lunchtime treats, Thumbelina desperately looked for a way to escape. If she tried to run, a warty toad foot would come down on her and she would be strictly guarded from that moment on. Better to appear as though she were going along with the wedding plans, she decided. Then she could somehow slip away and begin to climb out of the muddy hole. These toads couldn't even crane their necks upward, by the looks of them!

Thumbelina imagined herself shinnying up a vine into the branches of a tree or a bush. Nestled among those lilac or apple blossoms, she would wait for a kind butterfly or bird to carry her home. Maybe she would get back to the porch before her mother woke up.

Maybe her mother would never even have to know!

As Thumbelina's mind raced, she
tried to smile and tilt her head to one
side, the way she imagined a happy
bride would do. But it was not so easy to
fool the mother toad. She glanced at her
future daughter-in-law and knew imme-
diately that something was not right.

"Let's swim her out to a lily pad until everything is all nice for the wedding."

"Good idea, Mommy!" exclaimed Sylvester, taking to the idea of becoming a prison guard much more eagerly than he had to the role of bridegroom. "She definitely can't swim that far—I don't care how strong she is!"

"And then you'll marry her, don't forget that part," his mother gently reminded him.

The toads carried Thumbelina and her bed out of the muddy hole and into the dawn light.

*What a mama's boy,* thought Thumbelina bitterly as she watched Sylvester doing whatever his mother asked. She lay still while the toads put the cradle in the water and jumped in to push it. Her heart was so heavy with sadness that she was sure she would have sunk to the bottom if it hadn't been for her little walnut shell.

Thumbelina despised this ribbeting, web-footed pair of thieving amphibians. She loathed their bulbous, unbendable middles, their pompous, shiny flat heads, and their clownish pop-out eyes. Her life was over now, just when she had hoped it might begin. Thumbelina felt like she was being carried away in a coffin.

## chapter 6

"**O**ne, two, three . . ." Thumbelina's future husband and mother-in-law hoisted the walnut-shell bed onto a lily pad the way Thumbelina had seen her mother do with a bag of laundry.

"There you go, missy!" said the mother toad. "Sonny and I are going back now so's we can make everything nice for you two lovebirds in the bridal chamber." Abruptly, the pair shook the walnut-shell bed upside down so that Thumbelina, her diary, and her pen all fell out onto the cold, smooth surface of the lily pad, along with a petal and a few pieces of dandelion fuzz. Then mother and son grabbed the cradle and began swimming back toward the toad hole with it.

If only she had her bow and arrows, Thumbelina thought, narrowing her eyes.

She would take aim now, and maybe one of those toothpick arrows would pierce Sylvester's rubbery toad skin.

Hearing a conversation begin between mother and son brought Thumbelina back to reality. "A boutonniere is the flower you will wear in your buttonhole."

"It doesn't sound very manly."

"Nonsense, Sylvester. All grooms wear them."

Suddenly Thumbelina could see her future spread before her—endless days spent pulling the wings off flies and cleaning under the toad's stove. A tear ran down her cheek, and soon she was crying so hard that her whole body shook.

Invisible beneath the surface of the water, a school of tiny fish looked up.

They had heard the whole commotion and noticed with alarm how the lily pad was trembling beneath Thumbelina's sobs. Several poked their heads out of the water to catch a glimpse of her.

"Such a pretty little girl!"

*What a terrible injustice,* the whole school of fish thought in unison.

Thumbelina knew nothing of fish, so she had no inkling how deeply they would be affected by the spectacle of a small girl being married off against her will—to an ugly toad, no less!

The horrified fish began to nibble at the stalk of the lily pad beneath her,

taking tentative bites at first, because the rubbery stalk tasted awful. Then a ferocious anger swept over them—anger at every wrong that had ever been done to them by an amphibian. The whole school gnawed and gnashed with gusto until suddenly the slender stalk split in two. The longer end stayed stuck in the mud at the bottom of the pond, but the end attached to the broad lily-pad leaf began to meander downstream. The lily pad was a boat now, with Thumbelina standing on deck.

"What's happening?" the tiny girl wondered out loud.

In the glassy surface of the water, Thumbelina could see things she had only read about in books—cows on distant hills, a field of baa-ing sheep. An orchard of apple trees approached and then receded. Blinking tears out of her eyes, she began to believe it was true: somehow she had escaped.

The feeling of being free filled her with happiness.

From a mossy rock nearby, some baby beetles called out to their parents.

"Look! She hasn't got any antennae!"

The odd sight of a tiny human being drifting down the river on a lily pad began to attract attention from every direction. Butterflies flitted toward her. Birds sitting on eggs craned their necks to see. A spider, too shy to stare

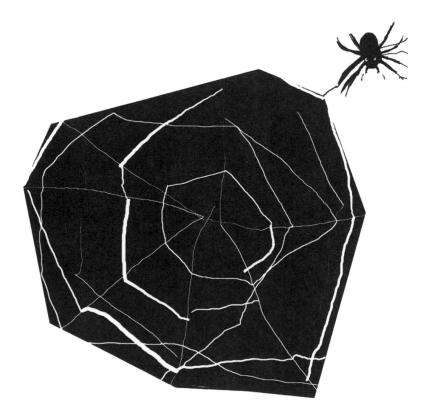

openly, gave Thumbelina a sidelong glance as she pretended to study her web for flies.

So this was the world her mother had kept from her. Seeing it now in all its glory, Thumbelina felt shocked, angry, delighted, and a little scared. Dragonfly wings shone different colors in the sun-light, frogs croaked, and birds sang.

What would *she* do? Thumbelina felt ready to find her place in this glorious world.

She sent a silent thank-you out to whoever or whatever had magically rescued her from marrying Sylvester the toad and living in a hole with his overbearing mother. Then Thumbelina reached into her pocket for her diary and began to scribble some thoughts, hoping that a similar miracle would send them to her mother:

Dear Mum,
This is to let you know
I didn't run away,
and
I wouldn't have. I love
Way
you too much. But
~~I am glad in a way.~~
~~I am happy~~
I am going to be
all right.
Love

chapter 7

W hen the lily pad got stuck among some tree roots, Thumbelina climbed to dry land. Clambering up the steep riverbank, she cut her knee. It was the first time she had ever seen her own blood. As she licked her knee clean, she tasted the saltiness. It thrilled her a little.

In the next few days Thumbelina got scratched, scraped, and bruised enough times that the novelty wore off. Her muscles grew sore and she tried to be more careful not to get hurt. A world where danger hadn't been chased away or fenced off had so many surprises, she realized. Often she was hungry or tired or just plain scared. She didn't have to follow her mother's rules, but there was a whole new set to learn—the laws of nature.

In the same way that Thumbelina used to read books, she now read the ground and the sky. She noticed fresh footprints and circling hawks. Her nose led her to wild raspberries and honeysuckle blossoms. She learned which animals to trust and which ones to watch out for. Partly it was a matter of size.

Creatures she could look in the eye—like grasshoppers and chipmunks—were not likely to hurt her, although now and then she'd get bitten by a hungry mosquito or gnat. While hawks were always eager to swoop down and eat a mammal her size, birds like bluebirds and swallows could be charming company. Animals that were strict vegetarians, like raccoons and beavers, were usually very friendly, despite the fact that they towered over Thumbelina. Fish eaters like the swans, ducks, and tortoises came off as a trifle snooty. They weren't interested in eating her, Thumbelina could be sure of that, but friendship with her kind didn't interest them either.

As she figured out these social nice-
ties, Thumbelina wove a complicated
web of alliances. In exchange for the
help she gave them gathering sticks
and building dams, beavers gave Thumbelina swimming lessons. She babysat
for bird children, and from their parents learned to find delicious nectar
and sip morning dew. A friendly rac-
coon helped her hunt for mushrooms.

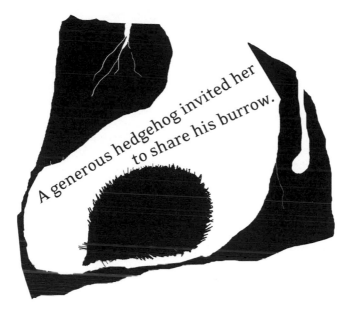

A generous hedgehog invited her to share his burrow.

A squirrel often came by to compare notes on where the best nuts were and to help Thumbelina crack open her share. The small girl who had once longed for company never felt alone.

But she had no one to love. Sometimes Thumbelina closed her eyes to be sure she could still remember what her mother looked like. And for her mother's sake, she tried to keep her hair tidy.

When she
missed her
mother, she
remembered
songs Anne Marie
had sung, and
it soothed her
to hum them.

Thumbelina still wrote in her diary.
She called Dorothy "Dot" now—a name
that seemed to suit her better. It was
good to have a friend to confide in.

Dear Dot, ➝.

    It's strange to ~~look~~ think back to ~~at~~ the things I used to write. I wanted to be able to go <u>out</u> and have adventures. Now I can have adventures, but I can't go home. I used to ~~get so mad~~ be so annoyed when ~~mum~~ my mother said, "Be careful what you wish for!" because I ~~loved~~ liked wishing for all those things. But now I guess I ~~kind of get~~ see what she meant. I feel like a different person in so many ways. More later. Still your best friend

🖐️ ⟵ Thumb

Thumbelina was so much in the habit of having her mother read the entries that she found herself compelled to write neatly and spell every word correctly. When she thought the words on the page might alarm her mother,

I am sharing a sleeping burrow with a hedgehog.

she would add some sort of explanation.

There's plenty of room for both of us. Besides, he's almost always asleep — except when he's eating.

There weren't words to describe many things she knew, so sometimes she drew pictures.

I think
a
badger

friendly

One chilly morning the pile of sticks and mud she liked to call her house had collapsed. Unlike the sleeping burrow she shared with the hedgehog, this had been above the ground and hers alone. There was no point in rebuilding it. It was winter now, and another storm would certainly knock a new one down as well.

chapter 8

The trees were nearly bare. There were no petals for blankets, and leaves were too brittle to offer any warmth. Thumbelina was cold nearly all the time.

The camaraderie of summer had ended too. Squirrels couldn't stop to chat; they were too busy hoarding nuts. Butterflies and bees were long gone.

Nights were lonely without the flash of lightning bugs and the hum of crickets. Thumbelina's days felt empty without birdsong. She kept secret from her diary how bad things were.

Every day it grew colder.

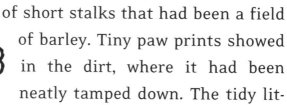

Sometimes, while searching for food, Thumbelina ventured farther from the river. One day she noticed a little hole in the ground amid a stubble of short stalks that had been a field of barley. Tiny paw prints showed in the dirt, where it had been neatly tamped down. The tidy little entrance made her think of her mother's wooden house with the boots lined up at the door. As she gazed at it longingly, big crystal flakes of snow fell from the sky, each one like a shovelful being thrown at Thumbelina.

"Excuse me,
dear, but this is some-
one's home," said the owner of a whis-
kered pink nose that poked out.

"I'm so hungry," Thumbelina heard
herself say.

A lady mouse in a checkered apron
appeared, shaking a rolling pin as if to
chase Thumbelina away. But when she
saw the shivering girl, the mouse took
pity.

"Well, I can't very well
leave you here like this.
Not with a storm on the way.
My goodness me.
You'd better come in."

Thumbelina felt ashamed, but she did as she was told and followed the mouse's tail into her small hole. It had been a long time since Thumbelina had been in any kind of a *real* house. There was a place for everything. Brooms, bowls, and nightclothes were all neatly tucked away. One little room was filled with soft fluffy things—milkweed and dandelion fuzz, and down. In the kitchen, pots and pans hung over the sink, beside which were neat piles of barley, rye, and wheat. Thumbelina could also see a parlor in the back, with a sofa and several comfortable chairs.

"What sort of mother lets a nice girl like you go hungry?" demanded the mouse as she handed Thumbelina a bowl of grain to eat.

Thumbelina just shrugged—which made her feel as if she were letting the mouse throw rocks at her mother. But with a snowstorm coming, this was no time to disagree with her hostess.

"Some fur would come in handy in this weather, wouldn't it?" said the mouse.

Thumbelina nodded in agreement.

"To be honest, I am normally not a fan of human beings," admitted the

mouse. "But you do seem a little different. I guess it's the size, isn't it?"

"Yes, I suppose so."

The mouse examined Thumbelina. "Hmmm," she said slowly. "Actually, I could use some live-in household help...."

"I'd be delighted," said Thumbelina, trying not to sound too eager.

"Without a tail to dust in all the crevices, you may not work out," remarked the mouse with a sigh. "Stay here tonight, and tomorrow I will do my best to train you."

Relieved to know where her next meal was coming from, Thumbelina slept soundly that night in the room full of fluff, lying next to her future employer.

After breakfast the mouse asked Thumbelina to put on a uniform with an apron. And the training began.

"I'd rather you mopped this way. No, do it like this. Here, I'll show you."

· 81 ·

At three o'clock a gentleman caller, the mouse's neighbor, was due for some afternoon tea.

"Mr. Mole is used to the very best," began the mouse fretfully. "We are quite good friends; in fact, if I wave my paw like this"—she batted imaginary gnats—"just vamoose and leave the two of us alone."

Thumbelina nodded.

"Because the mole's quarters are so much more roomy than my own, I like to give the illusion of a bit more space than I actually have," the mouse explained. "So right before Mr. Mole arrives, I pull those down," she said, pointing to the blinds above the windows. "It's just one of my little decorating tricks. It suggests that there may be corridors leading to other rooms."

Thumbelina did her best to smooth every surface as the mouse had shown her. She mopped and swept and polished the house from top to bottom.

"Not a bad effort," said the mouse, and Thumbelina thanked her.

"Shall I pull down the blinds?" Thumbelina asked, noticing that it was nearly three o'clock.

"*Blind* is not a word I *ever* want to hear used in this house!" snapped the mouse. "*Unsighted* is the correct terminology, and I'll thank you to use it."

Just then there was a knock at the door.

"Do I have to do everything *myself*!" exclaimed the mouse, making a helpless gesture. "Pull down those shades at once!"

As the mouse scurried to answer the door, her tail, no longer taut as a whip, became as flimsy and flirtatious as a feather boa.

"Oh my, is it that time already?" she asked the mole with a giggle, holding the door open for him.

"Three o'clock exactly," said the mole, bowing deeply.

In his gray felt hat, Mr. Mole was a most imposing gentleman. He carried a silver-topped walking stick that he used to help him feel his way around. Once inside the mouse hole, he removed his coat and handed it to the lady mouse.

As the mouse hung the mole's coat in the closet, she glanced at Thumbelina and pointed a claw in the direction of the kitchen. This was the signal

for Thumbelina to fetch the silver tray with the teapot and cups.

Mr. Mole's whiskers twitched uncertainly as he sensed the presence of another creature.

"Meet a poor orphan," said the mouse, presenting Thumbelina to the mole when the girl returned. "A teensy little human stray I rescued from a most terrible snowstorm!"

"Very pleased to meet you," said the mole, extending his front right paw.

"Delighted," said Thumbelina, touching her hand to his paw and dipping to a curtsy while the mouse nodded her approval.

chapter 9

"**H**ow do you . . . What brings . . . ?"

The mole was at a loss for the correct words to say in a situation like this (in which a small human being was temporarily being housed by a lady mouse she had not known prior to that occasion). The mouse rescued him:

"She is quite a good storyteller," she announced.

"Are you!" said the mole, turning to face Thumbelina.

The mouse nodded emphatically.

"Yes," said Thumbelina.

"Well, I think a story would be just the thing," said Mr. Mole, leaning back in one of the mouse's plush reclining chairs and putting his feet up on the ottoman.

With one eye on the mouse in case there were more signals, Thumbelina began.

"One day—well, one evening, really—my mother let me sleep outside, because I kept asking her...."

If the mole judged Thumbelina's mother for this oversight, he was too polite to say so.

"It was summer, early summer, you see," Thumbelina continued. "This was, I suppose, a few months ago. I was in the little bed my mother had made for me out of . . ."

The mouse, who was sitting in a chair beside the mole, stood up. With one paw on her hip and the other making circular motions, she indicated that Thumbelina should pick up the pace of her story.

So Thumbelina continued more quickly, careful to stop saying "you see," which, she realized, was rude.

After all, it was plain to see that the mole could *not* see.

The mole listened attentively, puffing and occasionally fiddling with his pipe. Now and then he would ask a question. "Did you notice if they had any provisions set aside for winter?" he inquired politely about the toads.

Thumbelina shook her head and was about to continue when she was prompted by more signals from the mouse. So she said out loud, "No, I didn't notice that, Mr. Mole. Unfortunately, no."

When Thumbelina described the moment the lily pad began sailing downstream, the mole became distraught. "Just when you think everything is going to work out," he said, putting his pipe on a side table and reaching into his pocket for a hand-kerchief, "all your hopes of wedded bliss and financial security—thwarted." He dabbed at the place where tears would have been.

"Such a shame," echoed the mouse.

"Do go on," said the mole.

Thumbelina described how she had drifted down the river atop the lily pad. When she mentioned the way the dragonflies' wings had glistened rain-bow colors, and how cows had stood on distant hilltops in dappled sunlight, the mole looked upset.

"Perhaps I am being thin-skinned," he burst in.

"I—I'm sorry," Thumbelina sputtered. "What is it?"

"I don't suppose you have noticed," said the mole, "but I am somewhat, um . . ."

"Nearsighted," interjected the mouse.

"Like she said," said the mole. "I am blind as a bat. So all of this glistening and dappling you describe is thoroughly hard for me to appreciate."

"*Impossible* for either one of us to understand," echoed the mouse. "And thoroughly insensitive," she hissed at her houseguest. The mouse then frantically waved her paws to indicate that Thumbelina should leave the room.

"She's only human," Thumbelina heard the mouse say after she'd grabbed the tea tray and awkwardly left. "And I wouldn't say you are thin-skinned, Mr. Mole, not at all. In fact, to me your coat seems to be most wonderfully thick." She paused. "Luxuriant, even."

The mole stood up, poised to go. From the kitchen Thumbelina saw the mouse hand him his hat. Sure now that she would be asked to leave the mouse's employ after her

terrible behavior, Thumbelina slipped a handful of grain into the pocket of her dress, which hung on a hook. She would be glad of this later, she thought, out there in the cold.

"Tell that small stray human that I thoroughly enjoyed her tale," she heard the mole saying. "Quite an imagination—for a human being."

"See you next week, then!" the mouse replied cheerfully.

Thumbelina hurried to make herself useful.

chapter 10

"Since you appear to be doing your best, I have decided not to let you go," said the mouse. "Mr. Mole is quite fond of your stories, clearly. But seeing as your housekeeping skills are rudimentary, I cannot offer you a salary."

"I think I understand better how you like things done," Thumbelina said.

"It took me a little while to learn, but now—"

The mouse motioned for Thumbelina to be quiet. She had another point to make. "I would also like to mention, since your mother apparently did not: if you are to stay on as a member of this household, you must keep in mind the finer feelings of others when you tell your stories. Not everyone can visualize things the way you can."

"Of course," said Thumbelina, looking at the floor.

"Tell me some more of your charming stories," the mole asked when he returned the following week. He sat down in the most comfortable chair and put his feet up.

Thumbelina closed her eyes to re-mind herself to use only words that had to do with hearing and smelling and feeling.

She managed to conjure up each scene beautifully.

"Then I held on to the butterfly and felt its wings carry me up...."

The mole was delighted. "I shall begin calling on Tuesdays, Thursdays, *and* Saturdays from now on," he announced jauntily as he was leaving.

The mouse was delighted too, but Thumbelina was not. Her days and nights were already so full of polishing and sweeping that she rarely wore anything but her cleaning uniform. Now things would be worse.

When the mole visited, Thumbelina no longer had to close her eyes to remember to leave the seeing parts out of her stories. The mole would settle down eagerly into the comfortable chair and listen attentively. As he left, he would tell Thumbelina, "I'll be wondering what happens next."

One afternoon the mouse scampered in with a trayful of tasty morsels just as the mole was telling Thumbelina,

"I believe you are that rare lady who can detect the substance that lies beneath."

As soon as he had left, the mouse turned to Thumbelina and said, "So nice of him to make that comment to you."

"Yes," said Thumbelina, picking up a broom to sweep the parlor floor. "I do my best to make the stories come to life."

"Have you felt how soft his coat is?" inquired the mouse pointedly.

"Of course not!" said Thumbelina, surprised.

"He's very handsome, don't you think?" the mouse continued.

"Well, um, I can't say I've noticed," replied Thumbelina awkwardly.

"An observant girl like you?" said the mouse doubtfully.

chapter 11

"**S**urprise!" the mole greeted Thumbelina and the mouse the very next morning.

Oddly, he wore no jacket over his suspenders. His shirtsleeves were rolled up and he appeared to be perspiring. It was an unscheduled visit.

The mouse rapidly checked herself to see that none of the nighttime fluff was sticking to any part of her fur coat.

Then she hissed to Thumbelina to pull down the shades.

"How lovely to see you!" said the mouse uncertainly. "However did you get in?"

"I tunneled," said the mole, a foolish grin on his face. "Come and take a look." And he showed them the passage he had dug connecting their two houses.

Holding out a front paw for each of them, he insisted that both ladies walk through it with him back to his house.

Seeing the mole less formally dressed made Thumbelina slightly uneasy.

"My family thrive on making underground thoroughfares," said the mole proudly.

"Spectacular!" the mouse cooed.

"Oops!"

The mole had tripped on a large object that was blocking the hallway.

"This wasn't here before," he complained, kicking it angrily.

"Oh! A swallow," gasped Thumbelina, surprised to see a magnificent creature lying before them, lifeless.

A shaft of light from above shone down on the bird; somehow it must have fallen through the crack in the dirt above them.

"Idiot!" said the mole, kicking the bird again. "I had it all perfect before."

"Not your fault!" soothed the mouse. "Our feathered friends can be so careless. Didn't look where he was going, did he?"

"If you two ladies could just kindly step to the side for the time being, I will see that this is removed later," said the mole.

But once the mole and the mouse had

walked ahead, Thumbelina fell to her knees to take a closer look at the poor swallow. Something about the set of his beak and the strong chest with its soft fluffy feathers touched her heart.

*I could end up frozen like this if I'm not careful,* she thought, and she patted the swallow tenderly where the mole had kicked him.

She could hear the mouse's laughter echoing farther down the passageway.

Quickly Thumbelina covered the bird with her woolen shawl and ran to catch up with the others.

"Could I carry the bird to our house . . . I mean, *your* house?" she asked the mouse carefully.

The two animals laughed.

"No room in my house for a dead bird!" replied the mouse.

By now they had reached the entrance of the mole's stunning underground mansion. In near-total darkness Thumbelina could make out vast rooms in all directions.

"You must have a tour!" the mole declared, squeezing Thumbelina's arm playfully.

"But I have chores I really must attend to," she explained, and turned abruptly to leave.

Thumbelina scurried back till she reached the bird, lying stiffly under her pink shawl. She didn't want the mole to remove him, so she dug the tunnel wider, scraping the walls with her fingernails. Then she rolled the bird into the crevice she had made and covered him with soil and dead leaves to hide him. Out of respect, she left his distinguished beak poking out.

"We don't belong down here," she said softly to the lifeless creature. "Another day I'll bury you properly."

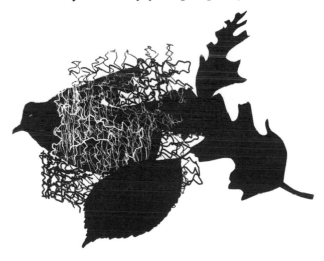

When she was back in the mouse hole, Thumbelina sat down to write:

Dear Dot,
　　We found a bird, a lovely male swallow. So beautiful it is hard to describe ~~him~~ Magnificent, but stiff and cold. I suppose he must be dead. I hate to use ~~that~~ the word dead because it seems so final. I want so much for this bird to be alive and able to fly again. ~~I don't know why but I do.~~

It was awful the way ~~the~~ Mr. mole kicked him and Ms. Mouse didn't ~~stop him~~ mind. They even laughed at him, which was so mean. I wish I had said something ~~or done something~~, but I just couldn't.
Does that ever happen to you Dot?
Your friend 4 ever
—Thumb

Thumbelina closed her diary and buried it deep in the pile of bed fluff.

It was not until much later that the mouse arrived home. By then Thumbelina had sorted and tidied the piles of grain, and every surface in the hole was smooth as satin. But the mouse seemed to be in an irritable mood. Thumbelina wondered whether a tattletale beetle had said something about her covering up the bird.

"Is anything the matter?" asked Thumbelina. But the mouse wouldn't answer. Instead, she excused herself, saying she was tired.

When she was sure the mouse was asleep, Thumbelina filled her pockets with grain just in case the mouse ordered her to leave the next day.

The next morning, the mouse told Thumbelina she had something important to say. She cleared her throat. "It's about Mr. Mole," she began gravely.

*Has he died?* wondered Thumbelina.

"He has decided to marry you. We spoke of it after you left yesterday. It has all been arranged."

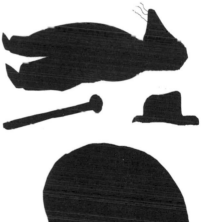

The mouse didn't pause to look at Thumbelina.

"Given your unusual circumstances, the mole has agreed to overlook the matter of a dowry.

We—Mr. Mole and I—will plan the event ourselves. Mr. Mole is used to the very best, so naturally this will be quite a grand affair. I will need to attend to a great many details. As a kindness to both of us, I hope you will not try to interfere."

## chapter 12

**T**humbelina listened
in stunned silence.
Wasn't it the mouse and
the mole who ought to
be walking down
the aisle? She
could see that
so clearly, and so could the
mouse. How strange that
the mole was blind to it.

"I am so happy for you," the mouse said flatly. "So very happy."

*If only I had known how to take care of myself, maybe put aside some provisions and dug a hole while it was still warm out,* thought Thumbelina.

"I have asked several spiders to come and spin a gown. It is something that I originally designed for myself," continued the mouse. "But I'm sure it can be altered for a person without a tail and so forth."

I will never see the sky again I will be buried beneath the ground forever.

Thumbelina realized.

Just then the mole breezed into the mouse hole via the tunnel.

"I am thoroughly thrilled, my dearest fiancée." He leaned over to give Thumbelina a kiss on the mouth, which she steered to her cheek.

"Thank you," she said awkwardly, her face flushing. "Oh, I forgot something." And she rushed out.

Burying herself in the bed fluff, Thumbelina tried to absorb what had just happened. She reached for her diary and pen and began to write.

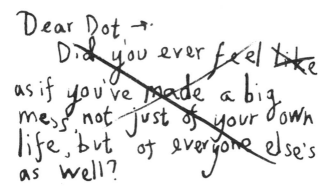

Dear Dot →.
Did you ever feel like
as if you've made a big
mess not just of your own
life, but of everyone else's
as well?

Mr Mole, the ~~blind~~
neighbor I have written to
you about, has decided
to marry me. It will
be a big celebration with

She lay still for a few moments, too
numb to find words. Then she had an
idea that it might be easier to write to
her mother instead.

Dear Mum,
   I am so confused. The
mole has decided to marry
me. ~~I am not sure *H~~
At least I will never have
to look up and wonder ~~about~~
about hawks. But I █████
going to miss see██████
the sky and so much.

She wished she could feel herself cupped in her mother's hand again. But she was too old for that now, and maybe this new life would be what her mother would want for her after all.

The thought comforted Thumbelina as she closed the book and put the pen inside. She put the diary back in the fluff near where she slept at night.

On her way back into the kitchen Thumbelina could hear the mouse and the mole discussing the wording of the wedding invitations.

"Request the pleasure of your companionship," said the mole.

"Of your *company*, I believe, is more correct," said the mouse.

Thumbelina stole a mint leaf and crept off to see the swallow.

*Is it wrong to place a sprig of mint on a bird's head when you are engaged to be married to another?* Thumbelina wondered. *Not if the bird is dead,* she decided. *It is a sign of respect.*

Clearing away the dead leaves and pulling back the shawl, Thumbelina embraced the poor bird. Both of them would soon be buried, she thought. At least the bird would be fortunate enough not to be buried alive. To calm herself, she sang a swallow lullaby that sounded like flowing water—quietly, so the mouse and mole would not hear it.

"Luaaah louiee. Ta tat a ta Wheeeee. Whoooo."

## chapter 13

The swallow seemed to shift slightly.

As Thumbelina sang a few more verses of the song, she began to see him in a new way. His wings stirred. Then his eyes stared into hers.

"Chirrup." The sound was weak at first, then grew stronger. "Chirrup!"

Thumbelina felt her heart jump with happiness at the life that had suddenly sprung up in the swallow. She leaned closer to kiss the top of his head, and he lowered his noble beak so that she could reach. Then she touched the soft feathers of his chest to feel the rapid pit-a-pat of his swallow heart. He looked at her weakly, as though still in a daze. When he placed a foot on her soft hand, Thumbelina felt a deep calmness settle over her.

"Everything will be all right," she told the bird.

"You are very good to me," he said. Then he wrapped her in his wings.

"I was flying, a little lower than the others," he continued, struggling to piece together what had happened.

"You have been unconscious for several days," Thumbelina told him.

"I must have torn my wing on that hawthorn bush." The bird paused. Pointing with a foot to the place where the mole had kicked him, he said, "It hurts here."

"I know," said Thumbelina, "but it's going to get better." As she spoke, she smoothed the rumpled feathers on top of his dear swallow head.

"Are we inside an egg?" he asked.

"No," Thumbelina told him. "But in a way, yes—just for a little while."

"Will I be able to fly south, to be with the others?" asked the bird.

"Yes, of course," said Thumbelina. "But first I will feed you the way your mother and father did."

"Have we always known each other?" asked the bird.

"Not always, but we will from now on," Thumbelina told him gently. "Look how quickly your strength is coming back! I am so happy," she said, and stroked his wings. "Stay a little longer in this tunnel—I mean, egg—while you collect your strength."

"Thumbelina!" The mole's voice startled them both. "Dearest, do come and help with our guest list."

"Who is that?" asked the bird.

"I'll be back," Thumbelina told the swallow. And with that she disappeared into the darkness.

"I was just admiring your tunnel!" said Thumbelina breathlessly as she returned to the mouse's parlor.

The mole laughed happily and patted her on the shoulder. While Thumbelina had been gone, the mouse's house had filled up with beetles and grasshoppers and snakes. Now they were all discussing menu choices and bridesmaids' shoe options. The homeowner was standing in their midst, looking somewhat alarmed. "I think we

should ask the beaver family, the porcu-
pines, some ducks, and definitely some
lightning bugs," Thumbelina chimed
in, trying to sound cheerful.

"That's exactly what *I* told him," said
the mouse defensively.
"By the way, I put
away your uniform.
You won't be need-
ing it anymore."

As the discussion
continued, Thum-
belina tiptoed
into the kitchen.

She filled a petal with water and
grabbed a handful of barley seeds,
then headed back through the tunnel.

Over the next few days a whirlwind
of wedding preparation was set in mo-
tion. Carrier pigeons were hired to

deliver invitations, and a tawny owl was prevailed upon to officiate.

"I don't normally do interspecies unions," he had objected.

"We are both mammals, though," the mole pointed out.

And reluctantly the owl had agreed.

"Do stand *still* so I can measure you," said the mouse with a mouth full of pins. Thumbelina was standing on a chair, trying not to sway as the mouse did her best to straighten out the hem of the wedding gown. In the mirror behind her Thumbelina could see a long trail of spider-spun silk.

Meanwhile, with each passing hour and each visit from Thumbelina, the bird grew stronger.

<br />
<br />

# chapter 14

Too soon for Thumbelina, the wedding day arrived. Her head was throbbing as she leaned out of the mouse hole one last time. She wondered if, after the ceremony, she would ever see daylight again.

It was happening so fast.

Already centipedes were arriving, hobbling in too-tight shoes, and butterflies were struggling to flutter in,

<br />

weighed down by magnificent jewelry. Muskrat ushers seated bats and mosquitoes, owls and chipmunks on opposite sides of the aisle. In a side room the mole's best man, a praying mantis, carefully straightened his bow tie. Even the dapper Mr. Mole felt a little self-conscious in his cummerbund as he practiced saying "I do" to himself. Crickets tuned their instruments.

And Thumbelina, in her spider-spun silken dress, waited for a signal to begin her fateful walk down the aisle. She wondered, *Does that music always sound so much like a funeral march?*

"Don't mess up my—" Thumbelina turned to see what creature was touching her hair.

She was surprised at the sight of the swallow.

He loomed above her. "I can't let you do this," he chirped in her ear.

"It has all been planned," whispered Thumbelina. Hundreds of eyes looked in her direction—eyes that could spot a droplet of nectar in bright sunlight, and eyes that could pierce the blackest night. Surrounded by dear friends and mortal enemies, she could see that each creature was waiting only for the ceremony to begin.

"*My* plan takes you up there," said the bird, pointing to the sky with his beak. "What is *your* plan?" he asked gently.

"I don't have a . . ."

The praying mantis slowly raised one leg—the signal for Thumbelina to begin walking down the aisle.

"Is that your path?" said the bird, looking at the narrow strip between creepy-crawlies and winged creatures, all dressed to the nines.

Just as the school of fish had known they had to nibble at the stalk connecting the lily pad to the mud below, Thumbelina knew she had to climb onto the bird's back. She had to put her arms around his soft feathery neck, just as the earth has to travel around the sun. "Are you strong enough?" she asked, suddenly recalling what an invalid the bird had been just days before.

In answer, the swallow leapt into the air and spread his wings.

An especially observant badger, a moth, and a bluebird all thought they saw a swallow take off with a silken trail floating behind it. A baby ladybug saw two pink arms around the bird's neck. But her mother told her to be quiet. "Shhhh, here comes the bride! Any minute."

They were flying now. Thumbelina looked down at the cluster of animals growing smaller. She hoped they would find something else to celebrate when they realized she had taken flight. She hoped the mouse would marry the man of her dreams; she hoped the mole would marry a woman who truly loved him.

As the earth curved, the sun grew hotter. They were heading south, and Thumbelina felt the rhythm of brighter colors, darker shadows, and louder insects. She held on tightly as they flew over mountains and through clouds. Flying lower, Thumbelina and the swallow could see tortoises lumbering across pink beaches toward turquoise seas. They flew and flew and flew, far

from Denmark, until at last they arrived at the ruins of an ancient marble palace overgrown with thick flowering vines.

"This is where I'm from," the swallow told Thumbelina as birds fluttered about and exchanged greetings in the warm afternoon light.

"Oh, look!" said Thumbelina, pointing to a white flower. The swallow swooped down to let Thumbelina slip comfortably into the welcoming circle of petals.

"I belong here!" said Thumbelina, feeling the echo of another flower from long ago. Overhead, the swooping and singing of swallows told her their journey was over.

"Will you be all right?" asked the swallow.

"Yes," said Thumbelina. "Thank you for bringing me."

"You gave me back my wings," the swallow told her.

"You gave me back mine too!" Thumbelina laughed.

"I will come and visit you tomorrow," said the swallow.

Thumbelina watched him swoosh up to the treetops in one swift movement, like the stroke of a pen. She looked out at the rosy tangle of vines, breathed in the scent of so many flowers, and felt a deep sense of peace.

Gazing in the direction of the setting sun, she saw something that startled her. A small human head was silhouetted against the pink sky–the head of a person as tiny as she was. Like her, the little man stood within a luxuriant white-petaled flower. On his head Thumbelina noticed a tiny crown. Her eyes feasted on his perfect face, his tiny hands, those little ears, the mass of golden curls.

He was looking at her.

For several seconds all either of them could do was stare. Nothing in the landscape existed for them but each other—not the other flowers or the palace's marble columns or even the setting sun.

As the little king began to travel toward her, Thumbelina saw that he could balance on a single strand of a spiderweb. Every stem and leaf and tree stump rejoiced when he touched it.

"I am king of all the flowers," the little king told her when he drew near, and Thumbelina knew it was true. Then he climbed into the shelter of her flower. And, shyly at first, they began to talk.

"I am so glad you have come," said the king awkwardly.

Thumbelina had never looked into such an impossibly beautiful face. The harmonious arrangement of eyes, nose, and mouth below his high forehead gave him a look of tenderness and strength.

"Oh," said Thumbelina, after too long a pause, "so am I."

As the sun went down in a blaze of color, the little king swept back his velvet cape and lifted the jeweled crown from his head, placing it on Thumbelina's. It fit perfectly. Then the little king knelt down within the white flower and, looking up into her eyes, said, "Be my sweet bride, dear Thumbelina."

Thumbelina smiled down at the little king.

"I don't believe Thumbelina is a suitable name for a queen," the little king told her gravely. "Instead, you will be known throughout the land as Queen Maia."

*Perhaps a pair of wings would make a suitable wedding present!* one fly thought as every living creature began to prepare for the tiny royal wedding.

epilogue

**E**xactly at this moment, the original story of Thumbelina ends.

Look.

THE END.

Now you know exactly what happened and can write a book report, if you need to do that, or count this as part of your summer reading list.

Nobody will mind or think any less of you if you just close the book and DO NOT READ ANOTHER WORD.

But, to tell you the truth, there is more. If you felt there was something forced about that ending, you were right.

Readers had already followed Thumbelina along rivers, into holes in the ground, and halfway around the world. Hans Christian Andersen, the man who made the story up, probably thought they

had traveled far enough and ought
to be allowed to put down their suit-
cases and rest. So, out of kindness,
really, he found a person of royal blood—
who was even the right height, and
good-looking—who wanted to marry
Thumbelina, so that everyone could go
home.

Except that after everything that had
already happened, Thumbelina would
*never up and marry* a man she hardly
knew—not if she *didn't love him!*—no
matter how many crowns he wore on
his head. You know that about her by

now, and so do I. (And those other people who stopped reading this book a few moments ago, they probably knew it too!)

Thumbelina admired the little king, was dazzled by him and thrilled that the two of them were the same size. But did all that add up to love? Well, no—no more than a bunch of notes will always add up to a song. And maybe she would have loved him, or maybe she should have loved him, or maybe she could have loved him . . .

But right now, right here in the story, she did *not.*

So instead of going along with the pretty story the little king sug- gested, Thumbelina said, "No, thank you."

"No . . . thank you?" asked the king. "What do you mean?"

"Well, I mean no. Thank you. I cannot marry you!"

"Pardon me," said the king. "I'm not sure I heard what you said."

"I am sorry, Your Majesty, but I cannot get married. To you," Thumbelina repeated in a loud voice.

"Why not?" demanded the little king, who was quite stunned. (Nobody had ever said the word *no* to him before.)

"Because . . . well, because— I, um, don't want to,"

And there it was; she had said it.

"I have other plans," she added.

The king pursed his lips and raised his eyebrows in a way that was not entirely distinguished. He opened his mouth, then thought better of it and closed it. And he decided then and there that he had better make some other plans too.

Thumbelina took a deep breath. She let the breath out slowly and wondered what would happen next.

At that very moment the swallow swooped down to check that Thumbelina was all right. And what Thumbelina said surprised them both.

"Take me home," said Thumbelina.

They both knew that she meant back to Denmark—to the faraway house where she had grown up.

It was the wrong time of year to fly north—too early, not yet spring. But the swallow loved Thumbelina deeply, and he knew that she had saved his life. He paused for a moment and cocked his beak to the wind.

A migrating bird feels many things, and the swallow felt all of them right now. Invisible threads connected him to the sun and the planets, to impossible dreams, to passionate longings, and even to the distant chirping of unborn chicks. He half-closed his eyes for a moment.

Then he replied.

"All right."

A cold wind blew straight into their faces as they headed north. Thumbelina wondered whether her arms were strong enough to hold on. But she didn't wonder whether she loved the swallow, because she knew she did. That part was easy.

The sun fell lower in the sky. Colors grew more muted.

Soon the river was right below them. As the bird flew lower, it looked like a narrow ribbon wiggling through fields and forests.

"Over there," Thumbelina whispered in the swallow's ear, pointing to her mother's rooftop.

The swallow felt Thumbelina's sharp intake of breath.

"Look, it's Mum in the garden!"

As the swallow landed, Thumbelina's mother looked up.

"Early for a swallow," she said. Then, seeing Thumbelina waving furiously, she looked more closely.

She didn't dare to believe what her eyes were telling her.

"Thumb!"

"Mum!"

The two of them were crying.

"I wrote letters to you in my diary."

"The witch told me you were all right."

Anne Marie gently cupped her daughter in her hand, the way she always used to.

Then the bird sang a sweet swallow song. It had a river running through it, and wings to make it fly—and maybe just the faintest smell of gunpowder. And Thumbelina joined in.

big thanks to

Anne Schwartz and Lee Wade

Georgia, Dexter and Ariel

Rachael Cole

Micheley Lifshen Reing

## about Hans Christian Andersen

**H**ans Christian Andersen knew about being different (and it wasn't just because he had an absolutely enormous nose).

His family was so poor that by the time he could go to school he was much older and much bigger than all the other children. As you might have already guessed, that meant he got teased a lot.

From what Hans knew, and from what he imagined, he made up lots of stories—stories like "The Little Mermaid," "The Ugly Duckling," "The Emperor's New Clothes," and of course, "Thumbelina."

Hans Christian Andersen was born in a small town in Denmark a little more than two hundred years ago.

He loved to make pictures by cutting up black pieces of paper with scissors, which is also how most of the pictures in this book were made.

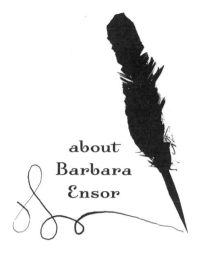

## about Barbara Ensor

Barbara Ensor is the author and illustrator of *Cinderella (as if you didn't already know the story)*, about which the *New York Times Book Review* wrote, "If God (or the fairy godmother, as the case may be) is in the details, then this [Cinderella] has some truly divine moments." Though Barbara has written for numerous publications, including *New York Magazine, Entertainment Weekly, Family Life,* and the *Village Voice,* she has yet to leave a bridegroom stranded at the altar.

Barbara's childhood, spent moving between England and America, made it easy for her to imagine the difficulties Thumbelina encountered in trying to fit into different worlds. Barbara now lives in Brooklyn, New York, and is the mother of two children, Georgia and Dexter, neither of whom is very, very tiny.

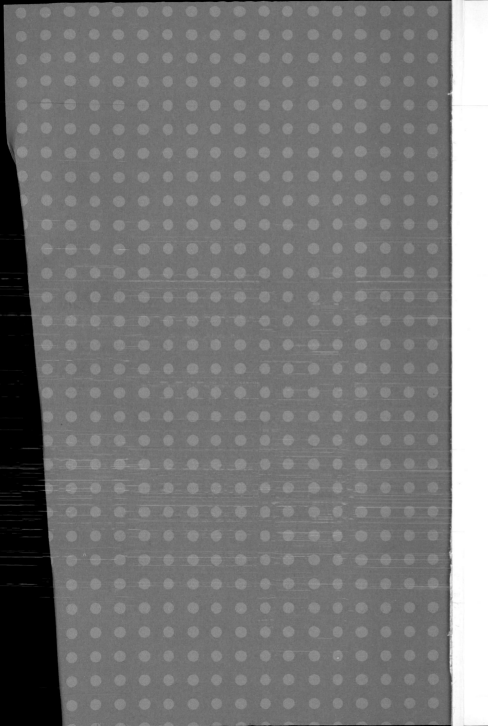

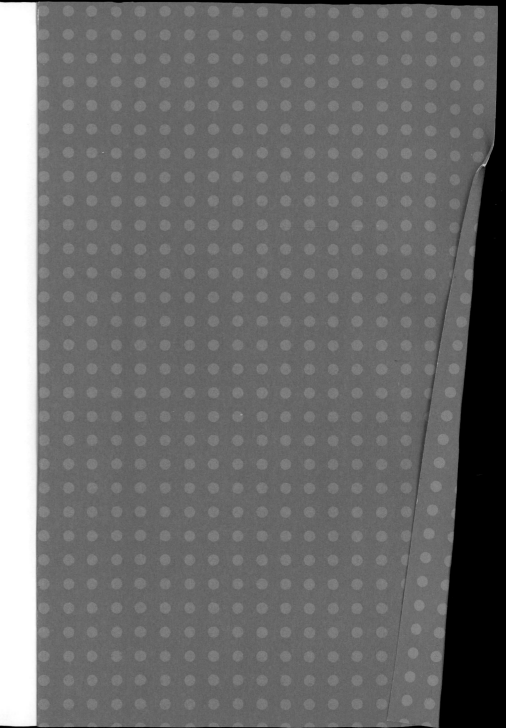